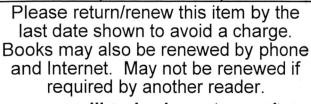

Please return/renew this item by the
last date shown to avoid a charge.
Books may also be renewed by phone
and Internet. May not be renewed if
required by another reader.

www.libraries.barnet.gov.uk

BARNET
LONDON BOROUGH

The TIDE SINGER

Eloise Williams

Illustrated by

AUGUST RO

Barrington Stoke

First published in 2022 in Great Britain by
Barrington Stoke Ltd
18 Walker Street, Edinburgh, EH3 7LP

www.barringtonstoke.co.uk

Text © 2022 Eloise Williams
Illustrations © 2022 August Ro

A CIP catalogue record for this book is available
from the British Library upon request

ISBN: 978-1-80090-011-0

Printed by Hussar Books, Poland

For Jo

CHAPTER 1

1895 – Carregton Crow

Our family have owned the funeral parlour in Carregton Crow and been the cemetery keepers for as long as history can remember. It's an important job. The town is small and everyone knows each other, so we all feel the loss when someone dies.

There are no bodies in the parlour today, so I'm free to make candles without being surrounded by dead people. At least when they are here Da weights their eyelids with coins, and I'm used to it – I've been around the dead since I was a baby. Still, it is good to have room to roll and melt the wax without being crowded.

It also means I can curse when I sting my fingers on hot beeswax, without fear of being heard by someone coming to pay their respects.

The warm smell of melting wax fills the air. I think proudly of how Da and I make sure people who have passed over are treated well. After the dead have been photographed with their family, we bring them to the parlour and lay them out gently. Da builds their coffins to size and I put ornaments and keepsakes in with them, then lay an embroidered cloth over their body. There is a neat pile of material on a shelf by the window waiting to be decorated with initials and patterns of stitches.

We take the coffins to our island cemetery by carrying them down the coffin tunnel. It leads from our back yard to the harbour where our boat is moored. The tunnel is narrow because smugglers dug it by hand many years ago, so we have to be careful not to bang the coffins against the edges.

As we sail to the island, I make conversation with the coffins, telling them what kind of day it is. I know the dead can't hear me, but it comforts their families to know that I do it, as letting go of a loved one is hard.

We bury them on the island and I leave blessings and candles at their graves so their resting place will look beautiful. The candles I'm making now are to replace the ones on the island that have been eaten by mice and other hungry animals. I feel proud when I think of the hard work and care Da and I have put into making the island a gentle place despite the worst of weathers.

Thinking of the storms makes me shudder. We have had so many and they have caused so much grief and devastation. Several local fishing boats have been lost, along with the men onboard.

The storms have been happening so often that everyone talks about the legend of the tide singers. People want an explanation for the relentless bad weather.

The tide singers are said by some to be an evil sea people who charm storms with their singing. They draw sailors in the wrong direction to destroy boats on the rocks. It is said that the tide singers hide in the waters around the cemetery island, but I don't believe a word of it. People like storytelling and exaggeration here in our town, where the losses at sea are plenty and there is no one to blame. Thankfully the last few days have been calm. I saw the fishermen setting out again this morning beneath a clear sky.

Peace fills our small parlour room while the day outside sings its song of gulls, clattering feet and hooves on cobbled stone. I love this time alone – humming and candle-making in the soft yellow light.

"Morwenna!" a woman's voice shrieks from outside. It rattles the window and my bones, and I spill wax on my wrist. I manage not to curse, as I know who it is before I even look up. She would give me a good cuff around the ear if she heard me swear.

Mrs Bussell enters the parlour as if she owns the place. "Where is your da? I have news of the utmost importance."

I don't rush from my work, because Mrs Bussell has very important news every day. She has made it her job to spread gossip since she was widowed. I need to be polite despite my peace being ruined, because she is the oldest person in town. Respect for our elders is hugely valued here. If you fail to mind your manners, you never hear the end of it.

I rise slowly. "Good afternoon, Mrs Bussell," I say, making my voice sweet and light, despite being irritated. "I will fetch my da for you."

Da is making repairs to the harbour door of the tunnel. I go out to the back yard, stand at the end of the tunnel, then cup my hands and yell into the tunnel's mouth.

"Mrs Bussell is here to see you, Da!"

I hear my voice echoing further and further until it fetches Da up from the dark depths.

"How delightful," Da says, popping like a cork from the darkness. He pushes his glasses up his nose and the glint of the lens hides his real expression. I know that he would always be polite, no matter what he was thinking, but sometimes when he is irritated with Mrs Bussell, I can read his real thoughts in his eyes.

We squeeze into the parlour, Mrs Bussell taking up much more space than us as she flusters and swishes. Then we wait as she wrings her hands dramatically.

"Well, Mr Jones," Mrs Bussell begins, "I want to tell you this news, but I am concerned it may be too fearful for your weak heart."

Da smiles. He is a kind man, kinder than me by far. "Mrs Bussell," Da says, "I would love to hear the news of the town, and my heart is as strong as an ox."

"What I have to tell you is serious, Mr Jones," Mrs Bussell says. "Please do not gossip it, for it is shared with only you."

Mrs Bussell shares her secrets with only us, then goes door to door to share them with everybody else. She takes payment from everyone for her news. It is her livelihood. It would ruin her if people ran around tattling tales faster than she did.

Mrs Bussell's face is aglow with delight, for there is nothing she likes more than to deliver bad news. She pauses dramatically, then whispers, "People have reported hearing eerie singing again."

My chest pounds suddenly. I'm almost certain I have heard strange songs in the air beyond midnight. They were bewitching, unlike anything I have known before. Enchanting sounds that made me want to go down to the sea in the moonlight. I had told myself the

songs were part of a nightmare or the place
between waking and dreams.

"Miss Howells heard them last night as she
took in her washing from the line," Mrs Bussell

went on. "And Mr Evans reported them while he was fishing before dawn."

Da nods and I lean in to listen to each detail. We swap glances. For once, Mrs Bussell's gossip is fascinating. We don't believe in the silly tales of the tide singers, but we are interested in discovering where the stories came from. We know that the storms are caused by atmospheric pressure and weather conditions from far across the sea, not created by mythical creatures.

But the singing? That I cannot work out. Was it my ears playing tricks on me? The wind howling across the shore? I must have imagined it. There is no other explanation. And yet Mrs Bussell says that others have heard it too. How can that be?

"That'll be three farthings," Mrs Bussell says, and holds her palm out. When she has told you her gossip, there is no way you can escape payment. Da has learned this by emptying many coins from his pockets over the years.

Once paid, Mrs Bussell leaves.

Da returns to his work and I return to mine in the parlour. The day moves into darkness. I've heard about the tide singers for as long as I can remember. There have been many reported sightings, but only ever by people who are alone. Someone battling a storm at sea, or seasick and likely to hallucinate. Those who have been at the ale have often seen them too.

People describe the tide singers so differently. Three-headed monsters with shark eyes and hair of eels. Beings made from the wisps of clouds and the swirling salt spray of the sea. Skeletons that dance on the waves, holding lanterns in their bony fingers.

Da and I have discussed the sightings often and shaken our heads at the vast differences in the descriptions of the tide singers. But the

singing? I'm almost sure in my heart that I
heard it too – no matter how I try to dismiss it.

I get back to making my candles to try to
distract myself from the creeping uncertainty.
I sprinkle poppy seeds into wax and add wicks.
I find myself humming a strange tune I did not
realise I knew.

CHAPTER 2

I have a sleepless night in which I listen for
songs and hear nothing but the restless sea
and wind. The next morning, we set off to the
island. We haven't been able to visit for a while
as our boat took a hammering in the last storm
and had to be repaired, so there will be lots to
do today.

The morning is fresh and cold. A sea of
silver bobs against a mackerel-grey sky. Our
boat, the *Memento Mori*, needs more repairs
before the teeth of winter bite in. It is
seaworthy for this journey, but the sail needs
patching and there is a leak in the hull which

has only been fixed temporarily and still lets water in. Da and I enjoy the slap of the oars against the swell of the waves.

Gravestones line the island and cormorants land on them to dry their wings as we pull into the cove. We each have our jobs. Da goes off to inspect the hut where we store some of our tools. It gets battered by the wind and the roof often gets blown off. I take trinkets and letters from family members to the graves, along with blessings of ribbons and feathers from me.

I pick my way across the grass, treading carefully so as not to twist my ankle in a rabbit's or puffin's burrow. Scattered seashells have turned the graveyard a colourful purple and blue where birds have dropped the shells to crack their hard outsides. A spider crab has been pecked clean, only its pincers left behind.

First, I clear the headstones of lichen and moss, then I scrub away the salt crystals covering the inscriptions, making the words sparkle.

I take a candle from my sack and place it in a glass jar. There is one at each grave so that the dead can have light should they need it. They are never lit and it is a silly tradition because the dead can't come back, but we've been doing it for so long that no one even questions it now. As usual some of the wax has been nibbled away by voles and mice, so the candles have to be replaced.

The wind from the sea crackles the October leaves. They scud over the gravestones and are plucked from trees bent low by the wind, like women cockle-picking. Seal pups mewl and kittiwakes chase each other in front of the salty clouds.

I make this place cheerful for when the darkest months arrive by standing fallen branches up in pots and tying jay feathers and blue ribbons to them. There are so many graves it is impossible to tend to them all in one day, but I try to say hello to as many as I can.

It helps to fight the loneliness I get from a long day at work here.

"Hello, Jeremiah," I say to one gravestone. Jeremiah lived to sixty-six. I can't imagine how it would have felt to be so old.

I collect flowers and plants. The scent of them fills my head with memories of so many days spent here on this island. When we get home, they will be crushed and put into one

of our tonics for good health or scattered into candles to make scents for funerals.

No matter what the season, flowers and plants grow on the island. I spike myself on the needles of gorse and bleed on the last of the red campion's pink petals.

I catch a strain of music on the air and jolt up, looking around with alarm. I scan the sea and the shifting tides, searching for something evil coming to get me. Mrs Bussell's rumours are playing tricks with my mind. I keep imagining that I hear the song I found myself humming in the parlour yesterday.

A short-eared owl hovers in the sky and swoops down to lift something small. A weasel or a rat is meeting its death. I hear Da's hammer striking far off, and the constant suck of the sea pulling at the edges of the island. I remind myself that there is nothing to fear here except an occasional bird dropping. I turn my attention back to the graves, decorating them with seashell patterns.

"Hello, Violet," I say. She died of cholera.

"Hello, Mrs Grubbins." Influenza took her.

As I work hard, the air suddenly switches direction. When you have lived this close to the sea all your life, you know to take note of changes like this. Da's hammering has stopped and the sky is silent. There is a storm coming.

I gather up stray flowers and scurry back along the island path. Da is waiting in the *Memento Mori* and we set sail hurriedly. The storms can be fast and violent here, even without invented beasts, and the island is no place for the living when one hits.

CHAPTER 3

We tether the boat in the harbour back at
Carregton Crow and rush into the tunnel
towards home. The clouds begin to bleed on the
horizon and thunder growls in the distance.

The rain of the storm is hard and turns
swiftly to hail. It hits me like bullets as I put
the bar down on the tunnel's top wooden door
to protect us from the surging sea. Then I
make certain the windows are fastened and the
shutters locked.

We sit by the fire and eat, then Da reads
a book aloud. When we go to our beds, the

wind makes the house rock as if it is at sea. It howls down the chimney, blowing soot onto my freezing feet. I lie there listening to the creak of our funeral-parlour sign on its hinges, mistaking it for the sounds of a spellbinding song.

*

I must have fallen into an uneasy sleep for I'm awoken by a banging so loud it can be heard above the rage of the storm.

Da has woken too. His candle throws long ghostly shadows across the walls. I pull a shawl around me and rush after him. Rain lashes in as Da opens the door and brings with it three of his friends. They're drenched to the bone and soak the flagstones.

"The storm has taken boats," Mr Owens tells us. "The *Tempest* and *Seren Nos* have been blown off course."

Mr Lewis from two houses down shouts from the doorway, "Crew from the boats are missing too. Everyone must join in the search."

Da pulls on his oilcloth coat. There is no time to dress properly beneath it. We have lost too many at sea over the years. Empty spaces under gravestones where bodies should be dot the cemetery island.

"Be careful, Da," I say. A rescue mission is dangerous. I don't want him to go, but I must be brave. He heads out into the yowling wind and I use all of my weight to shove the door hard shut.

I pace the floor this way and that. I fetch my sewing basket so that I can embroider a cloth to fill the time. But my hands are shaking too much to thread a needle.

A sudden hollering from outside makes me jab myself. The door bursts open again and this time it's Thomas Pettigrew, one of the local fishermen. He carries a girl in his arms.

"Washed up," Thomas says. "Caught in a net. Stranger." He can barely breathe and I clear a space for him as fast as I can to lay the girl down. She looks half-drowned, but her groans show me there is hope.

"I'll take care of her," I tell Thomas. The reputation of our family's health tonic is known far and wide, and this girl is not yet dead. Thomas has brought her to the right place.

I take a green glass bottle down from the shelf and drip its contents into the girl's mouth. She groans loudly but doesn't wake. Her lips are blue and I know I must get her warm while the tonic takes effect. Using a linen cloth, I pat gently at the girl's soaked tresses of hair. The sea must have wet her right through because her hair simply will not dry. I pat it and rub it softly with the cloth, then wring and mangle it forcefully. But no matter how much water I take off, her hair still drips and a puddle collects on the floor. Eventually, I give up.

I wring the soaked cloth over the sink, then hang it near the fire to dry. When I turn back, the girl is sitting up straight and staring at me.

"I'm Morwenna," I say. I unwrap the shawl from around my shoulders and step towards her. She puts her hands up in front of her face as if I'm going to attack her. It shocks me. I have never had someone scared of me before. "I mean you no harm," I say. "I'll look after you."

The girl doesn't reply, but she lowers her hands enough to watch me closely. I gently toss the shawl towards her. She ducks away from it, then picks it up carefully and sniffs it with suspicion.

She is wrapped in one of the fishermen's coats, and I mime taking it off and putting the shawl on, hoping she'll copy me. I pass her one of my dresses which has been hanging near the fire to warm, then I turn and stoke the fire so that she can have privacy. The flames flicker and hiss.

I sneak a glance and am happy to see she has put the dress on.

"Let me get you some broth to heat you from the inside," I tell the girl, and swing our iron pot out over the coals. I notice its contents are thin. We keep some fish just inside the back yard door where it is coldest. I fetch some and search for the sharp knife Da uses to gut them.

I look up from rummaging through his crate of tools and see that the girl is dangling a whole fish in her mouth and down into her throat. She brings it out in one deft movement with only the bones and spine left. I'm shocked. She must have been famished with hunger.

The wind screams suddenly and one of the shutters crashes open. I jump almost out of my skin and am distracted from this strange sight. I must save the glass in the window.

The force of the wind almost knocks me off my feet as I go outside. The shutter breaks free of its hinges and hits my hand hard as it flies into the street. My cry of pain is scooped up by the sky and hurled over Carregton Crow. This storm is the worst I have seen. The rain falls so hard I fear it will pockmark my face. I am so afraid for my da out there in this. I must keep busy so that I don't give in to weeping.

Back inside, the girl watches me carefully as if I might pounce at any moment. She spits out thin white fish bones, one by one. There are no fish left in the bucket. Rooted to the spot, I stare as she picks her teeth with one of the sharper bones, then throws it onto the pile. Perhaps she's had a bump to the head that's making her act so strangely? This is not normal behaviour.

The water from her hair still falls and there are pools of it all over the floor. I take a mop from the scullery and try to soak it up. I must keep busy to take my mind off Da.

When I go near the girl, she whimpers. She is afraid. I hold the mop upside down and pretend that it is a person. I waltz around the parlour with it. When the girl smiles, I smile too, then go back to mopping because the floor is becoming slippery.

No matter how much I mop, the floor still seems to be wet. Irritated, I give up. The girl copies my annoyed face and puts the shawl around her head. She ties it so that it stems the flow of water from her hair.

I smile to show I'm grateful, then press my hand to my heart as the wind howls even more loudly at our door. I peek through the window and am horrified to see that the storm outside is furious – violent enough to sink a thousand ships.

"Da," I wail, unable to keep my worry inside. I pull my hands into fists to try to control myself, but my sobs just keep on coming.

The girl makes a strange screeching sound to match my own. The shock of it stems my tears. She raises one of her long fingers and points to the water bucket. She must be thirsty.

Wiping my nose on my sleeve, I try to tidy myself, then dip the ladle into the bucket and fill it with water.

The girl takes the ladle. I turn from her so that she might not see the hot tears that are now sliding down my cheeks again. I will let her drink and then put her into my bed to sleep while I wait for Da's return.

I'm startled by another strange noise from behind me – a moaning high-pitched sound. I turn and realise it is the girl. Her head is low above the ladle and she begins to sing. Her song is so familiar. It is the same one I heard from my bedroom in the middle of the night. The same song I caught the sound of at the cemetery island. I'm certain of it.

I'm frozen to the spot. Her mouth forms words I've never heard before. Haunting words that are so long they seem impossible to fit in your mouth. Words so short they are barely more than a peep. The sound is hard to describe.

The words are like shingle rolling on the sand, the chatter of pebbles as a wave drags them out, the swoop of a tern as it flies above the shallows. I picture white horses cresting the

tops of waves, salty spray sparkling in the sun, the emerald swirl of the sea.

The girl brings the ladle towards me. When I look into it, the water shimmers like mercury. I gaze more closely and see that something has begun to appear in it. Tiny boats! How can this be?

Transfixed by the sight, I watch the boats as the girl's singing gets louder and reaches a crescendo. I recognise our boat – the *Memento Mori*. What magic is this? I'm horrified and spellbound at the same time.

The girl stops singing abruptly and the storm outside suddenly halts. Shafts of silver moonlight glitter through the window and into the room. I try to close my mouth, but it remains an O. The girl reaches out one of her bony hands and pushes my bottom jaw back up. In the ladle, the water is still and the tiny boats glide across its surface, then they disappear.

There's only silence as the girl looks at me and I gawp back at her. She is a tide singer. I am shocked to my core. If the stories are true, she can control the sea with her words, make the tides change direction, bring up treasures from the deep. My whole body shakes with disbelief. Magic can't be real, can it? And yet here it is in front of my eyes.

Can I learn to use it? What must it feel like to have such power in your words? My mind rushes with thoughts and questions, and my mouth has fallen open again. I can feel myself gulping at the air like a fish on land.

At that moment Da walks in, completely unharmed.

"It is a miracle!" Da says, throwing his arms up triumphantly. "The storm just stopped. And the boats and their crews have all been found safely!"

I rush to hug him, not minding his sopping clothing or how cold he is.

"Da, it is not a miracle," I say. "It is magic."

But Da doesn't hear me and spots the strange girl in our house.

"Who is this?" Da asks.

I'm about to tell him that she is a tide singer when something stops me.

"She was washed up on the shore, Da," I explain. "A stranger. She can't speak our language. We can take care of her until she is well and then find out where she lives."

My face burns with unspoken truths, but I want to keep this secret to myself. I want to learn the tide singers' magic, and if I reveal what the girl is, Da will think I'm mad or tell me it is too dangerous to let her stay here.

Da is used to unexpected patients being brought to the parlour, so he doesn't question the truth of what I say.

I glance shyly at the tide singer and hope she doesn't do anything to give my lie away. For now, I want to keep her to myself.

CHAPTER 4

In bed, I only wriggle and itch. The tide singer
sleeps close to me and because I'm trying not to
move, every part of me wants to. I look across
at her, bathed in moonlight now that the sky
is clear. She looks every bit like an ordinary
girl – except that her hair is still wet and every
time she snores, a cloud of salt erupts from her
mouth.

I want to prod the tide singer awake and ask
her lots of questions, but that would be rude of
me. Instead, I thrash about a bit and yank at
the blankets, hoping this might wake her. When
that fails to work, I sigh as loudly as I can, over

and over. Eventually I forget my manners and give her a sharp prod.

The tide singer wakes up with a start and snaps at my outstretched finger with her teeth.

"I'm sorry," I say. "I just wondered if you could tell me a bit about your ..." I want to say magic, but I worry it will sound greedy. "Life."

She moves her head from side to side as if I am a puzzle. I try to think of ways to make myself clearer.

I attempt acting the question out. I point at her, then pretend to dive beneath the water, swimming through the cold air of my room. I look around and hold up my arms as if questioning what is around me in my imaginary undersea world. It makes the tide singer laugh. Eventually, after pretending to be a leaping dolphin, I collapse in giggles onto the bed.

We kneel and face each other. The tide singer reaches out and takes my hands in hers, then presses my fingers to her temples. It is such a peculiar thing to do, but I trust her. I close my eyes.

She is sending pictures through my fingertips – I see her diving beneath the waves and to the seabed. I have no idea how. I open my eyes and we are still inside my room and it is night, so I close them again.

I follow her with my mind and we swim over the skeletons of shipwrecks. Huge shoals of silver fish part to let us between them. The world is like a deep blue sapphire around us and the sun a shimmering gold above the water. A curtain of seaweed seems to block our way, but we swim straight into it. Fronds tickle our arms and legs as we burst out of the other side and into a dazzling blue again.

Here there are underwater caves. Tide singers dart in and out of them. So many, I

think this must be where they live. A strange shape lies on the seabed and suddenly I know where we are. The strange shape is the bell we lost from our boat, the *Memento Mori*, a few years ago. The bell sank too deep to rescue it and its heaviness means it won't have been moved far by the motion of the sea. That means that these caves must be under the cemetery island. It is beautiful to see this world that I have been so close to and yet had no idea was here.

Something strange and fearful looms out of the darkness. It is a net from one of our fishing boats. The tide singer tries to pull me away, but I'm not fast enough. I'm trapped in it. Struggling just tangles me more. There is no escape. I can't breathe. I'm caught like a fish. Tangled. It hurts. I need to be free.

Alarmed, I open my eyes. I understand now. That is why the tide singers are causing the storms. They are driving the fishermen away to save themselves from their nets.

"I am so sorry," I whisper. And I mean it.

We lie down. The tide singer burps, releasing a cloud of salt that explodes in front of the moon, then falls to sprinkle my face. The burp has a stinky fishy smell which drifts around the room until I'm wrapped in sleep.

*

I wake as dawn begins to sneak its glow into the corners of the room. I get up. My feet are silent on the cold flagstones as I make my way along the corridor.

In the parlour, I sit next to the fire, which has been banked with stones to keep it from going out overnight. The ladle rests in the water bucket, glinting in the light of the embers.

I will just have a small drink of water and then get on with my morning chores.

But temptation grows inside me as I pick up the ladle, prickling the hairs on my arms and whispering suggestions into my ear. I want to control the sea. Just to send out a tiny ripple. Nothing that will cause harm. I tell myself that if I manage to do anything at all to the water in the ladle, I will put it down immediately.

At first I can't hit the notes because I'm whispering so as not to wake Da or the tide singer, but soon I get close to the tune she was using. I keep singing the notes longer than she did as I try to remember the words. No one has heard the tide singer's song as closely as I have, I'm certain of it, so why can't I get the words right? They clunk and clash as I try to copy them. They come out wonky and strange on my tongue.

There is something wrong. The water in the ladle begins bubbling and boiling with alarming

41

speed. I stop singing, but the water continues moving, swelling up at one side and starting to slop over the edges of the bucket. A thunderous roar from outside fills me with horror.

Rushing to the window, I see a wall of water building on the horizon, so huge it will smash our town to pieces in seconds. I try to drop the ladle, but it is stuck to my hand by some invisible force.

At that moment the tide singer bursts into the parlour and grips my wrist tightly. She pulls the ladle to her mouth and sings until the water becomes flat and the rushing noise that fills my ears is calmed by her tongue. When she has finished, the tide singer flops to the floor in exhaustion.

The huge wave outside has disappeared, but I'm horrified to see Mrs Bussell's face pressed against the window pane. Of course, she must have come here to spin her tale of events during the storm to rake in as much money as possible. I should have been more careful.

Mrs Bussell's eyes are as big as saucers. She hammers at the door, shouting and screaming.

Already people are rushing from other houses, coming to her rescue.

"We must hide you," I say to the tide singer. I try to drag her out towards the tunnel in the back yard, but she is too tired to move. I think the singing has drained her.

"What is going on?" Da calls out, shocked from his sleep. He goes to help Mrs Bussell at the door. He opens it too fast for me to stop him. I try to shout, but I'm frozen by fear and no sound comes out – perhaps because my voice is afraid of the harm it has already done.

Mrs Bussell falls into the room, screeching so shrilly I have to cup my hands over my ears. "She conjured up a wave to kill us all."

I screw my eyes tight at the accusation and I wait for hands to arrest me. But when none come, I open my eyes to see that everyone is staring at the tide singer, not me. Da tries to calm Mrs Bussell, but she is having none of it.

The others look on with faces of confusion and amazement.

Mrs Bussell moves about manically, clearly enjoying the audience. She points at the girl on the floor and shouts, "She is a tide singer!"

CHAPTER 5

There are gasps, and the words tide singer are spoken again and again. The crowd stream in through the door and gather behind Mrs Bussell. They seem afraid at first, but soon realise there is strength in numbers. They are angry because of all the damage the storms have caused and now they have someone to blame.

I try to stay next to the tide singer, but I'm shoved aside. More and more people push in front of me, shouting angrily. Soon I'm at the back of the room and can hardly see the tide singer past the raging mob.

I must tell them the truth. That it was me who conjured up the wave and that the tide singers are only protecting themselves from fishing nets by driving the boats away. I try to make my way through the crowd, but I'm swept off my feet.

I'm not strong enough to push to the front, so I crawl forward between their legs. I get glimpses of the tide singer, who is cowering on the floor. I reach out for her hand, but I'm yanked back.

"Do not touch her," Mrs Bussell shrieks above the hubbub of noise. "She may have more evil magic we know nothing of."

Biddy Thomas prods at the tide singer with a walking stick and her daughter faints. The crowd surge forward again to get a better look and Da is almost knocked over.

"No," I shout, but no one can hear me above the crowd's roar of fury. Da tries to stop them, but they use some of his rope to tie the tide singer's wrists, shouting orders all the while. It is petrifying.

I follow the crowd as they carry the girl out. Mrs Bussell orders them to take her to the town museum. The prison is no longer used, since it was damaged in the last big storm when a tree fell through its roof. The crowd climbs the hill to where the museum overlooks the sea from a high cliff.

"We'll take care of her from here," Mrs Bussell says. "You can all go home to await further instructions." She and her cronies take the tide singer inside and lock the door behind them. Five of the townsfolk are left on guard and the rest slink off, some grumbling, some excited by what has occurred.

I sneak to the back of the museum. There is a grate on the side of the wall which you can spy through without anyone knowing. I discovered it almost by accident when I was eavesdropping on a town council meeting. I like to be informed.

I can see Mrs Bussell and her cronies between the slats. They are gathered around the tide singer. She looks terrified. They look terrified too. I press my ear to the metal and hear them discussing what to do with her. Mrs Bussell wants to charge money for people to be allowed to view her and demands half of the income for trapping the girl herself.

"What about the other tide singers?" Thomas Pettigrew asks. "If we keep this one imprisoned, surely they will cause storms to drown us all."

"How will we be able to fish now?" a voice asks. I can't see who it is from my view through the slats. "We can't risk taking our boats out."

"We need to give this careful thought to avoid the tide singers' wrath," Mrs Bussell says, her voice cruel. "Be careful. Don't go too close to her. She might set her magic on you."

I shift position and watch as they put the tide singer into one of the display cabinets. She presses her hands to the glass on all sides as if she doesn't understand its invisible force. She is gasping for air and freedom. Mrs Bussell turns the key in the lock and hangs it on a chain around her waist. I feel my insides rising up my throat. I must do something. This is all my fault! I feel my face burn with shame.

Da will help me. I know it.

*

When I get to the parlour, Da is sitting at the table, his face a picture of shock. He has never believed in the accounts of the tide singers and has always put it down to wandering imaginations.

"Where have you been, Morwenna?" Da asks me. He stands so fast he knocks his chair to the ground. "Are you hurt?"

"We need to save the tide singer, Da." I'm panting for breath from rushing and panic.

"You need to sit down and explain what has happened here." Da's voice is stern.

I tell him about the tide singer as fast as I can. I start to tell him about causing the wave myself, but shame makes my mouth open and shut without words and I can't face his disappointment. Instead I tell him that there is no time to waste.

"They've locked her in a cabinet," I say. "They're talking about keeping her. They have imprisoned her, Da. They might never let her go." I stop for breath and Da holds his hand up to signal that he needs to think. He picks the chair up quietly and places it back at the table, then sits and presses his fingertips together like the steeple of a church.

"We need to go, Da," I say. "We need to get her out of there. Talk to Mrs Bussell and the others. Change their minds."

Da unhooks his spectacles from behind his ears and rubs at his eyes.

"We can't go against the whole town, Morwenna," Da says.

"But, Da."

"We can't simply decide what is best for everyone," Da goes on. "People are angry. People are sad that they have lost so much in the storms."

"But it wasn't her fault," I say.

"Perhaps if you had told me straight away that she was a tide singer, we could have returned her to the sea before anyone found out." Da hooks his glasses back and shakes his head slowly. "Now it is too late for us to help her, I'm afraid."

There is a lump in my throat the size of Wales. I can't believe I was so stupid.

Leaving Da in the parlour, I go to my room. The pillow is still wet where the tide singer lay her head last night and there is salt scattered across the blankets. I lie down and weep at my own stupidity. When there are no tears left, I decide on a plan.

I will wait until nightfall and rescue her alone.

CHAPTER 6

I wait until I hear the sound of the midnight bell tolling from the town square, then I get out of bed. I have not slept a wink. Da's snores are coming at a comforting rate and I creep out of the house in time with them. The floor threatens to freeze my feet to it with each careful step.

I have never gone against Da's wishes before, but I know in my heart that I have to. I must release the tide singer and take her to the sea.

The streets aren't lit at this time of night, and the shadows lengthen and hide who knows

what. I try desperately not to think about murderers as I sneak up the alleyway.

Mrs Bussell's house is in darkness. I need to steal the museum keys. I'm hoping that she won't have locked her own door. No one does in Carregton Crow unless there is a storm. I'm relieved to find it opens easily.

Mrs Bussell sleeps in a room towards the back of the house with her keys beside her. I've seen them when I've delivered health tonics to her for ailments of old age. I make my way carefully down the hallway and stop at her chamber door. It's slightly ajar and I can see she is asleep. Next to her are the keys, gleaming like treasure.

I take a deep silent breath, grit my teeth and tiptoe into the room. Mrs Bussell mumbles and turns, a feather from her pillow drifting onto her nose and irritating her. She flaps at it but doesn't wake.

I keep my eyes on the keys. One step more and I'll have them. But then I trip over something and my stomach flips as there is an almighty yowl. I have fallen over Saundersfoot, Mrs Bussell's miserable cat.

I duck down into a ball as Mrs Bussell yells at the cat to be quiet, and I wait until she seems to have settled again. Saundersfoot stares at me with hatred and I stare back, pleading with him.

When I'm convinced Mrs Bussell is properly asleep, I pick up the keys gingerly and sneak out of the room as silent as a shadow. I can hear Saundersfoot mewing behind me, trying to wake Mrs Bussell. I never liked that cat.

It is bitterly cold as I make my way to the museum on the clifftop, but the sky is clear and full of stars. The icy air turns my breath into clouds that hang heavily for a few moments before vanishing. A howling wind would be welcome now to hide my noise, but tonight the weather lets me down. Even the sea is quiet, as if it too is afraid.

My hand trembles as I try to push the biggest key into the lock and turn it. It is old and will not fit at first. I have to use both hands. Eventually, I'm in.

Monsters loom from the shadows inside the museum. The glass eyes of a giant rat gleam at me, and birds hanging from the roof by iron hooks rock on their strings. There is a mermaid, which looks small and ridiculous in the day. Everyone knows it's a whale's tail sewn to a doll's head, but it seems freakish now. Every creak and tick of the old walls tell tales of terror.

The tide singer is hunched into a ball. As I approach, she starts in shock, then sees it is me and cries tears of what looks like blue glass. I press my hand to the display cabinet so that I leave a print behind. Let it be known for ever it was me who let her go.

"I'm so sorry," I mouth.

The cabinet unlocks with a painfully loud noise. I wait, quiet as a church mouse, my heart

pounding. No one comes. No faces appear at
the window.

Once the cabinet is open, I see how much
the girl has wilted in these conditions. It is
worse than I had imagined. Her hair is brittle

and snapping, and her skin is cracked and dry. Solid blue tears slip from her chin and scatter on the floor of her cage. I recognise these – I have found similar glass tears strewn along the sands. The tide singers must have been crying a lot, which makes me furious. It gives me new determination.

"I'm taking you home," I say.

The tide singer cowers away from me. I don't blame her.

"I promise you," I say, and put my hand on my heart to try to make her understand. "I will take you to the sea."

There is an oil painting of a faraway ocean on the wall and I point to it, then to her, then hold out my hand and hope.

It is her turn to be brave. The tide singer is too weak to stand alone, so I help her up. With my arm around her waist, we stagger to the door. Time is against us. Mrs Bussell could wake at any moment. The tide singer's breath rasps close to my ear as we move as fast as possible through the dark streets.

"I need to fetch some tonic for you," I tell her. "It will give you strength."

I know the tide singer doesn't understand what I'm saying, but I use a soothing tone so she won't be afraid. At the funeral parlour I open the door as softly as I can and close it behind us carefully.

"What is going on?" Da demands as he stands at the fire. His voice sounds different to anything I have heard before and I realise he is afraid.

"I had no choice, Da," I say. "She is dying."

There is a moment where nothing happens. The coals in the fire glow and crackle. The night waits and watches at the window. I feel my panic ticking past the seconds. We are caught like statues here in the act of escaping. The tide singer struggles for breath and almost falls from my arms.

It moves Da into action. He grabs a bottle of tonic and hands it to me. I'm so grateful he is going to help us. I feed her two large spoonfuls. It will take time to have an effect. Da opens the door to the back yard and beckons us through.

"We must be quick," Da says. "Let's take her to the water."

We rush outside and into the tunnel. Strange sounds screech through it from the sea, the scent of seaweed rising to us. The tide singer is getting more and more exhausted. Her breath comes in rasps and I have to take more of her weight. We are only part way down the tunnel when we hear the church bells ring out. That only happens in an emergency. Someone knows. We must have been seen.

"You go," Da tells me. "I will stay behind in case they come to the funeral parlour to search." Da turns and is swallowed into darkness as he heads back up the tunnel.

CHAPTER 7

It takes so much time for me and the tide singer
to stumble to the bottom of the tunnel together,
but we get there at last.

The sea is frothing black and hissing as if it
is angry.

"Do you have the strength to swim?" I ask,
and point to the water, making a swimming
motion. The tide singer shakes her head and
rests heavily on my side. I don't know what to
do. The townspeople will capture her unless I
think quickly.

The tide singer points to the *Memento Mori* and then points in the direction of the cemetery island.

"Yes," I agree, knowing what she means. If we make it to the island, I can hide her until the tonic has taken effect. But the idea scares me.

I shouldn't be taking the boat out. Da thought I would simply return the girl to the sea or he would never have left us. Our boat needs more repairs, but I will have to risk it. If it sinks, at least the tide singer will have a chance. I can't think about my own safety when I have caused so much pain.

I help the tide singer into the *Memento Mori* and take the helm. I have never taken the boat out alone, but I have been at sea for at least half of my years. There is hardly any wind, so I use the oars to push out.

We pass through the mouth of the harbour and I can already see lanterns dotting the alleyways. I pray the people holding them won't catch us. There is nothing else to do but hope. I cut across the black waves, heading for the island, wishing for a miracle.

The wind picks up a little but whistles through the holes in the sail. The temporary patch on the leak isn't working any more and the water is ankle-deep.

To my horror, I see the boats of the townspeople appearing behind us. We are not going to make it. Salt blurs my eyes and I can taste blood where I must have knocked myself somehow. Our small boat is no match for theirs. The townspeople draw closer still. I can't see my way to the island.

"We need to go faster," I say. I think I'm crying. I don't know what to do. There is no one to help us. We are alone.

I look back at the tide singer, who is lying at the stern of the boat. *Please*, I beg the sea and the stars. *Please help us.* The tide singer opens her mouth and retches. I think she is going to be sick, but then an almighty noise comes from her throat.

Her voice howls out of her. It catches on the spray and zings upwards, tossed to the moon and out over everything I have ever known.

There is a sound in response, so strange and eerie that my heart stops beating for a moment. I look back to the tide singer, but it is not coming from her. It is coming from all around us. Filling our ears. It is louder and more piercing than anything I've heard in this world.

All around us, tide singers begin to appear in the water: ten, twenty, thirty, perhaps more. Singing at the tops of their voices. A wind starts so suddenly that the boat rocks and almost tips over. The waves grow in seconds and whip up strange clouds of water from the sea. *Monsters*, I think in my panic. This is what people saw.

We are being blown in the wrong direction, back towards home. I have lost control of the boat and the waves are growing to a gigantic size around us. The moon is hidden by clouds now and a thick churning fog is appearing from nowhere. Behind us the sea boils, spinning the other boats as if they are no more than matchsticks and halting their progress. In front of us is the island somewhere, hidden by monstrous waves and swirling fog.

"I can't see," I say. My hair whips into my eyes and lashes my face. We'll crash on the rocks if we don't pull into the cove on the right sea path.

"Help!" I scream to the dark sea and sky. I can't see the island. All hope is disappearing.

Suddenly, there's something ahead. I'm not certain what it is at first, but then I see it more clearly. A light. Tiny and insignificant at first – but soon it is joined by more lights. Now I can see a glow shimmering beyond the fog.

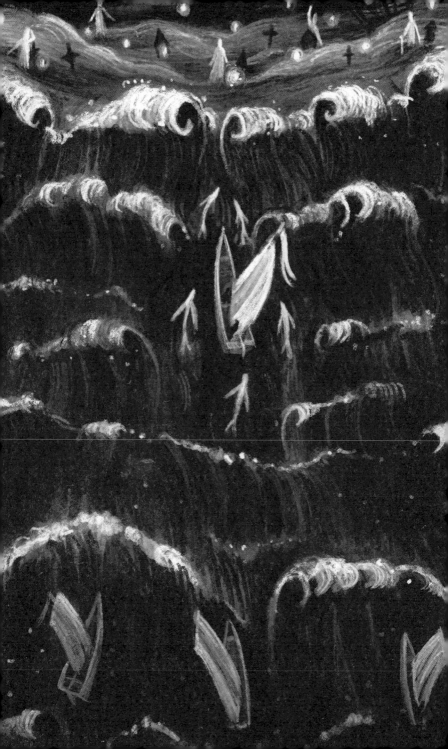

The tide singer comes up behind me and points at them.

We take the helm together and steer the *Memento Mori* towards the lights. As we emerge from the fog, I realise what they are.

More and more lights are appearing all over the island. It's the candles I left on the graves – they have all been lit somehow. They sparkle and guide us through the darkness. Who lit them? Ghosts? For a moment I think I see Jeremiah, Violet and other figures in the gloom. Surely not? But who else?

We dock and tie the boat tight in the cove. The sea still rages and I'm beside myself with worry. Worry about the people of my town, and worry about Da. What happened to him when he went back up the tunnel?

The tide singer is still too weak to swim, so I help her out of the boat and she sits heavily on the sand. There are no ghosts to be seen now, but the candle flames still flicker brightly in their little glass jars.

The bottle of tonic that Da gave me in our escape is remarkably unbroken. I hold it to the tide singer's lips so that she might drink again. She needs to regain her strength so she can escape.

We are partly sheltered here in the cove, but out on the water it is perilous. I look out, despairing at the storm the tide singers have created. The townspeople following us on their boats won't survive this. Lightning flashes the sky.

"Please," I say. I drop to my knees at the tide singer's side and plead with my hands. "Can you help them?" I point out to their boats.

She doesn't move to answer. I don't know if it's because she is too weak or if she wants to get revenge on the people of my town.

"I know what they did to you was unforgiveable," I plead with the tide singer. "But they are my people. My family and friends. I promise you I will keep you and the other tide singers safe if you just let them live." I try to act out what I mean with gestures, but I'm panicked. I have no idea if she understands what I'm trying to say.

The tide singer still doesn't move to help me and I let out a scream of frustration and fear. She grabs my hands and puts them to her temples as she did before. It's different this time. I don't only see things. I hear things. Her language. The song she sings. We sing it together. She channels the words through me. Our combined voices are so powerful, and the words are so clear. We are asking the other tide singers to calm the waters. I can see it. A vision of my people and hers living happily together. There is enough sea for all of us and plenty of fish. Perhaps we can learn things from each other. Celebrate our differences instead of being afraid. Our voices in harmony are telling the tide singers that we can live in peace.

When we have sung the last word, I open my eyes and the storm has been replaced by stillness. Candles glow all over the island and stars scatter the sky. The townspeople's boats slide across the smooth waters towards us and tide singers bob in the shallows.

Laughter bubbles up and bursts out of me. It's not that our situation is funny. It is a mixture of emotions. I'm not surprised – I have seen people laugh till they're bent over double at funerals.

The tide singer looks at me as if I'm mad. She smiles. Her strength is returning. We help each other stand and I hold her hand while we wait.

When Mrs Bussell and her cronies land at the cove, we are united and ready.

CHAPTER 8

Mrs Bussell looks shaken but fearsome here in this eerie light.

A few of the other townsfolk stride up behind her. Most have turned back to the harbour.

"Where is my da?" I ask. I can't think of anything else until I know he is safe.

"Locked in the coffin tunnel," Mrs Bussell says. "He will be released as soon as we have her back." She points at the tide singer, who flinches but stays strong.

I'm relieved that Da is not injured, but a cauldron of emotions bubble inside me. "This must stop," I say. "The townspeople and the tide singers need to find a way to live together."

Mrs Bussell laughs now, but her laughter isn't pleasant. "Why should we when they have wrecked our boats and created such horrifying storms?"

"They've done it for a reason," I say. My voice quakes and my fingers tremble against the tide singer's, but I stand my ground. "They have been getting caught in our nets. Injured. They created the storms to drive our boats away from them, to save their people."

Mrs Bussell scoffs at this and points towards the tide singer next to me. "I suppose that's why she was creating a wave so large it would wash our town away?"

I know I must confess. "It was me. The wall of water. I tried to sing their song, but their language isn't made for humans," I explain, trying to convince them that it was all my fault.

"A likely story," Mrs Bussell shouts. "They almost killed us just now. Can you explain that?" Waves begin to appear around the tide singers again. Their voices circle us, low and violent.

"Yes, I can explain." My whole body is shaking now. With fury and hope. "They *almost* killed us. Think about it. They could have sunk all our boats today, or any other day. They could create a wave so tall it would wash us clean from the island at this moment if they truly meant us harm." I feel so tired, but it's now or never. I have to make them understand. "The tide singer stopped the wall of water I created. Don't you see? She saved us all."

"What are we supposed to do? Let her go?" Mrs Bussell guffaws with laughter and encourages the others to join her.

I know why she is like this. Mrs Bussell has grown bitter with grief. She's had to become hard to survive. She needs money because there is so little to be made by a woman alone. She sees an opportunity to change her fortune by capturing the tide singer. But I have seen how beautiful life can be if we all live together. The tide singer's vision showed me that we can all live in peace. I need to make Mrs Bussell understand that it is the only way.

"Yes," I say. "Let her go. We'll let the tide singers have the space around the island to swim freely, without fear of being caught in our nets."

Mrs Bussell sneers. "But we've always fished these waters."

"But the tide singers are only asking for a small, safe piece of sea around the island. We can fish anywhere else. In return, they won't cause any more storms." I look at the tide singer, hoping that I have understood her wish correctly. "We will be safe and you, Mrs Bussell, will be the saviour of our town for putting this plan in motion."

I'm hoping this flattery will work. Mrs Bussell needs others to see her as important, to fill her emptiness inside.

"They may even build a statue of you in the town square," I add, but then worry I have overdone it. I bite the end of my tongue to stop myself from saying more.

There is a long pause as Mrs Bussell's face contorts. She's weighing out how the options stack up. "How do we know we can trust them?" she asks.

"We don't know for certain," I say. My argument ends here. I can't predict the future. I may be wrong and we might not be able to live together. I'm too tired to try any harder. I've given it everything I have. "But we can hope."

I have a thought which might just end the argument.

"I don't know about you," I say to Mrs Bussell and the townspeople behind her, "but as much as I love the cemetery island, I don't want to be laid to rest yet."

There really is no choice. If we can't come to an agreement now, the tide singers could drown us on our way home. Mrs Bussell realises it and the rest do too. A grumble ripples between them as they understand our dilemma.

"The tide singer can go," Mrs Bussell states, knowing everyone will listen because she is the eldest. "But we will be watching closely to make sure that they keep their end of the bargain."

Mrs Bussell doesn't want to be seen to give in completely. I understand that. She moves aside and gestures to the others to do the same. The tide singer hugs me quickly, then dives into the water. A song of celebration lifts and trills

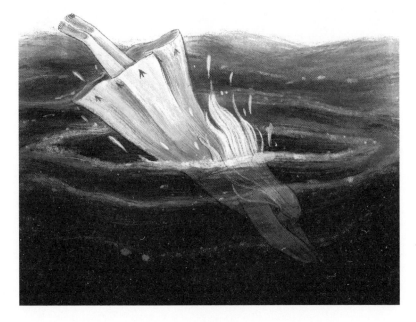

like a million turquoise butterflies, then all the tide singers slip beneath the waves. My dress floats up to the surface.

"What are you waiting for?" Mrs Bussell says to the others, giving orders like always. "Let's head back before we freeze to death. And I'll hear no talk about a statue of me in the town square."

She means the opposite of course. Everyone understands that this is an order to erect a statue in her honour.

I feel for Mrs Bussell now that she doesn't have the gossip of the tide singers to sell. As we make our way to the boats, I call her back.

"I have a secret," I whisper. "It is only for you."

I'm hoping this is a kind thing to do and will keep Mrs Bussell in business. "We have no idea who lit the candles, but I think I saw the ghost of Jeremiah."

Her eyes shine, and I know she'll make the most of this.

CHAPTER 9

There has only been one storm since we made our agreement with the tide singers. That is to be expected when you live by the sea. Nature cannot be changed.

Da whistles as we make our way to the island to carry out our day's work. It has been just over a month since the night we changed our fate. The fishermen take care to steer clear of the island when they fish, and the tide singers are happier. It will take a while for the trust to build from both sides, but it's a very hopeful start.

Mist rises as we approach the cove and oystercatchers squabble and scurry over the sand. Da goes off to search for any storm damage and I set about my tasks speedily to stay warm.

No one has explained how the candles were lit that night, but Mrs Bussell is doing a roaring trade by spinning her stories. For me, it is simple. When I needed my island people, they helped me. The candle wicks aren't even burned, but I know what I saw.

I bid good morning to Verity. She died of smallpox. And Anwen, who died in the mines. On each grave I leave a sprig of mistletoe and a pale blue ribbon for cheer.

"We will be singing in the town square this evening," I tell them. "You're welcome to come along. Carols by lamplight is one of my favourite things."

Eventually, the sky becomes striped in orange, pink and lavender, and cold stars start to fleck the heavens. I go back to our boat to meet Da.

We sail out gently and the tide singer appears alongside us, as she always does now, and sings one of her songs. It's impossible

to copy it unless she shares it with you. Her language is the music of the sea and the notes of a turning tide. The tide singer's words bring warmth and hope and shine most beautifully when they are out in the wild and free.

Acknowledgements

Huge thanks to the brilliant team at
Barrington Stoke, most particularly
Victoria Walsh, Ailsa Bathgate
and Julie-ann Murray.

Thanks to August Ro for the illustrations
that so beautifully bring the story to life.

Thanks too to my agent, Kate Shaw,
a wonder of a woman.

Our books are tested
for children and young people by
children and young people.

Thanks to everyone who consulted on
a manuscript for their time and effort in
helping us to make our books better
for our readers.